Cambridge Early Years Mathematics

Learner's Book 2B

Alison Borthwick & Cherri Moseley

Contents

Note to parents and practitioners					3

Block 3: Working and playing together					4

Block 4: Wonderful water					18

Acknowledgements					32

Note to parents and practitioners

This Learner's Book provides activities to support the second term of Mathematics for Cambridge Early Years 2.

Activities can be used at school or at home. Children will need support from an adult. Additional guidance about activities can be found in the **For practitioners** boxes.

Children will encounter the following characters within this book. You could ask children to point to the characters when they see them on the pages, and say their names.

The Learner's Book activities support the Teaching Resource activities. The Teaching Resource provides step-by-step coverage of the Cambridge Early Years curriculum and guidance on how the Learner's Book activities develop the curriculum learning statements.

Hi, my name is Mia.

Find us on the front covers doing lots of fun activities.

Hi, my name is Rafi.

Hi, my name is Gemi.

Hi, my name is Kiho.

Block 3

Working and playing together

2D shapes

Tick and say.

Tick (✔) the shape that does **not** belong in each row.

Look at each shape in the row. What is the same? What is different?

For practitioners
Encourage children to identify which shape is different from the others in each row and explain what is different about it. Invite children to name each shape in the row. Challenge children to arrange, draw or print their own row of shapes for a friend to find the one that does not belong.

3D shapes

Tick and say.

Tick (✔) the shape that does **not** belong in each row.

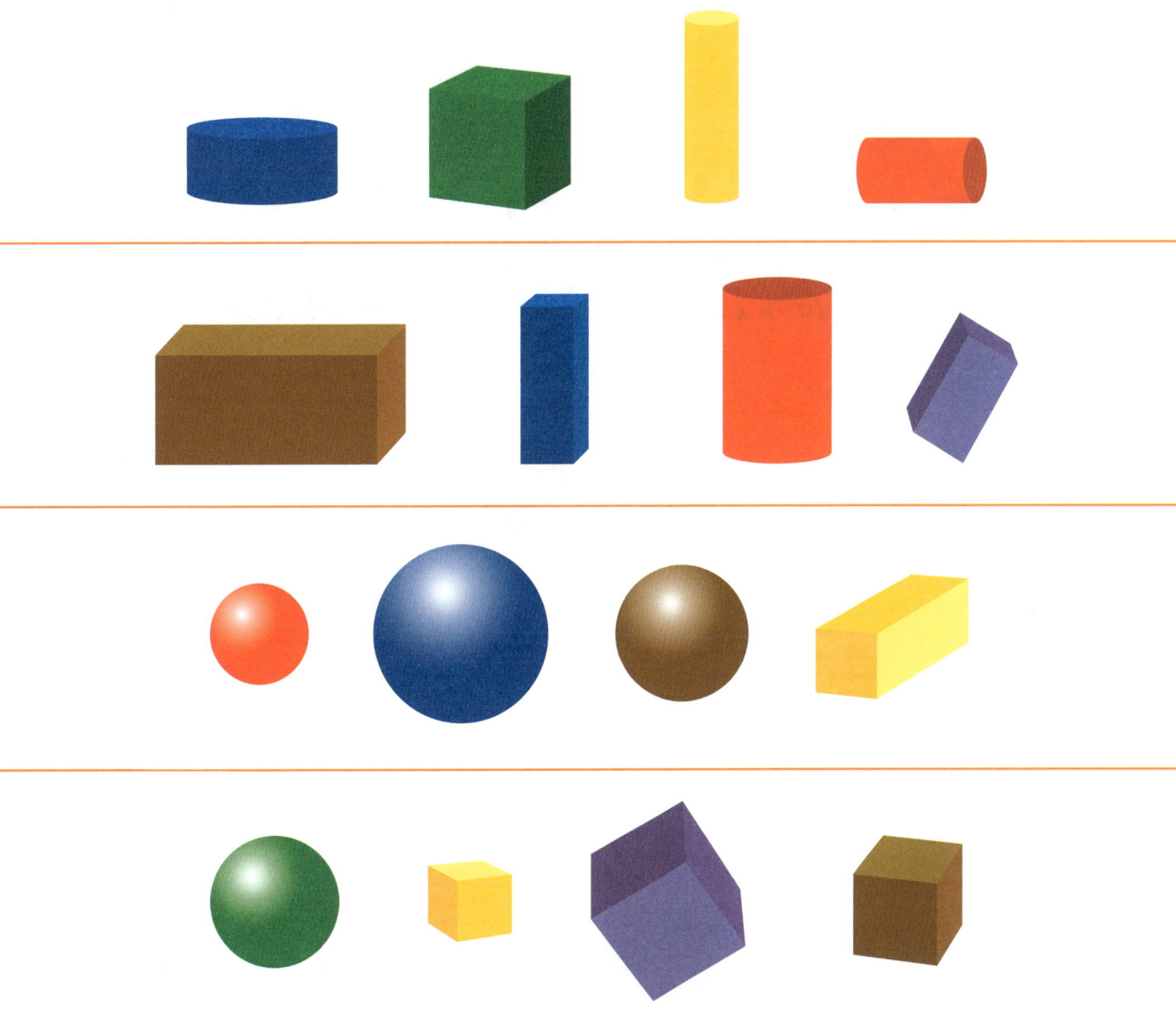

> **For practitioners**
> Encourage children to identify which shape is different from the others in each row and explain what is different about it. Invite children to name each shape in the row. Challenge children to arrange their own row of shapes for a friend to find the one that does not belong.

Shape picnic

Match and say.

Draw lines to match the objects to the shapes.

For practitioners
Encourage children to say which objects in the picture look most like the sphere/cube/cuboid/cylinder at the bottom of the page, then draw lines to match the objects to the shapes. Challenge children to match everyday items to a set of 3D shapes.

Circles or not?
Sort.

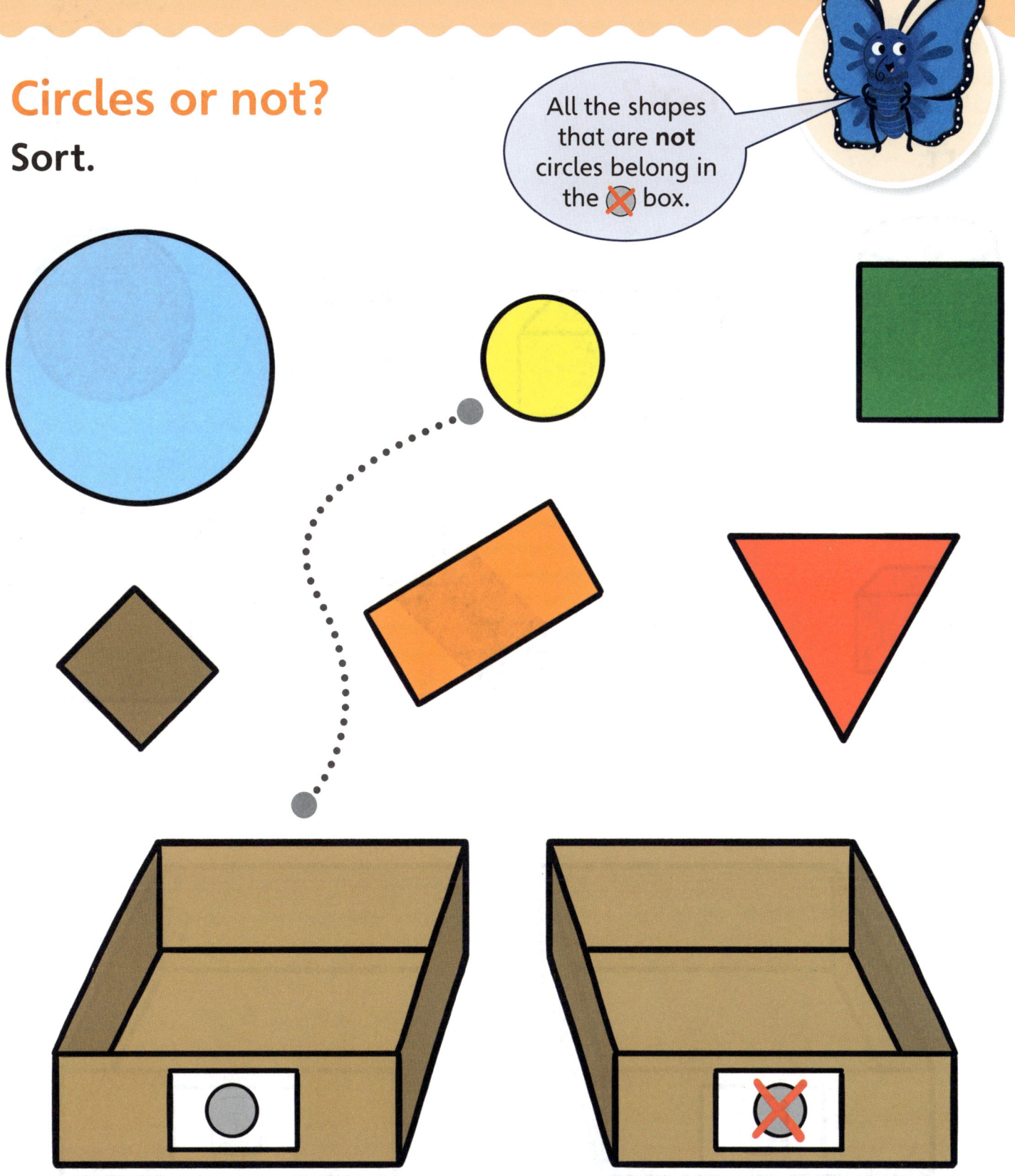

All the shapes that are **not** circles belong in the ⊗ box.

For practitioners
Encourage children to draw a line from each shape to the correct box. Some children will find it helpful to hold a circle and compare each shape with their circle. Challenge children to draw some shapes to add to each box.

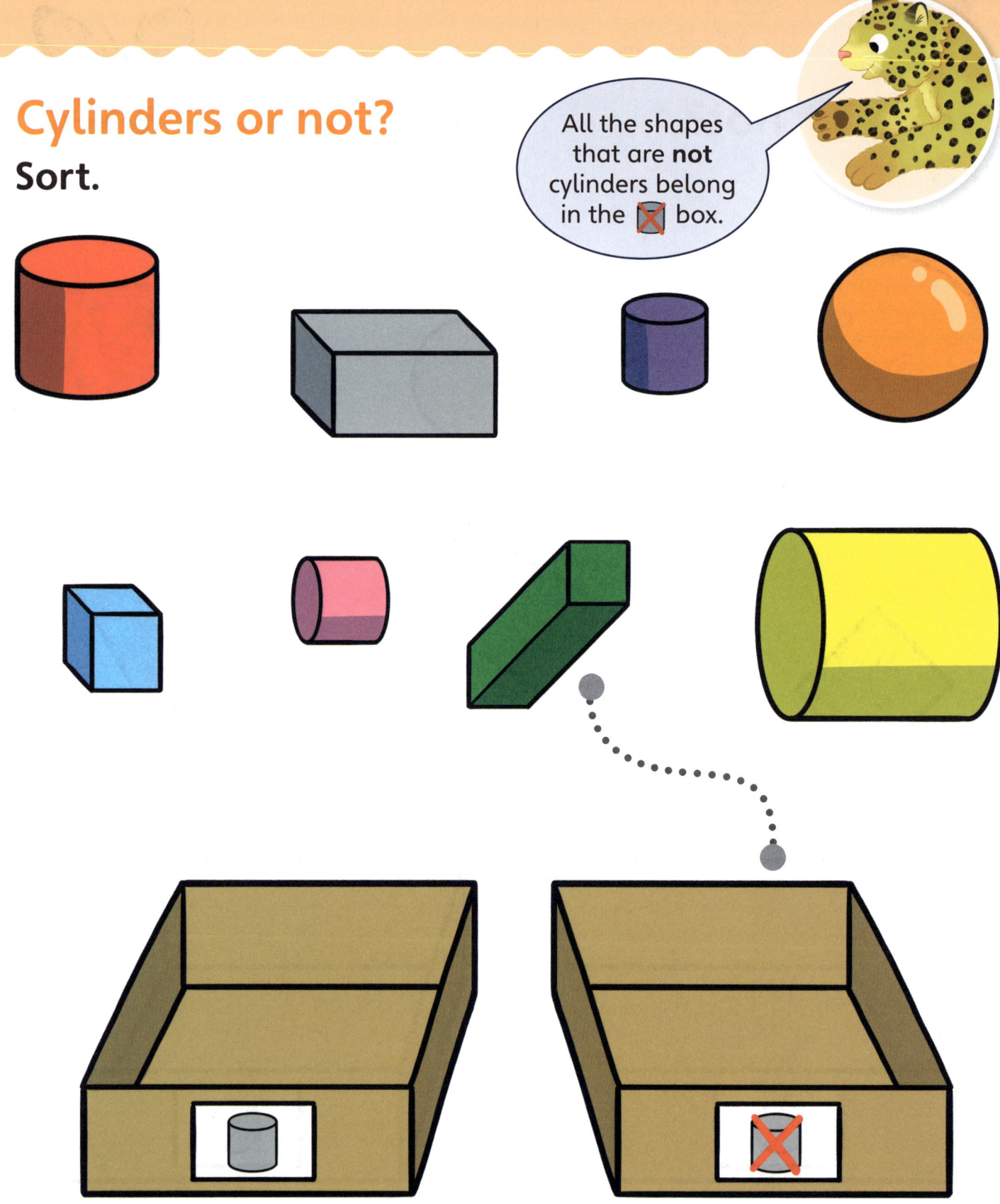

Shape sorting
Sort.

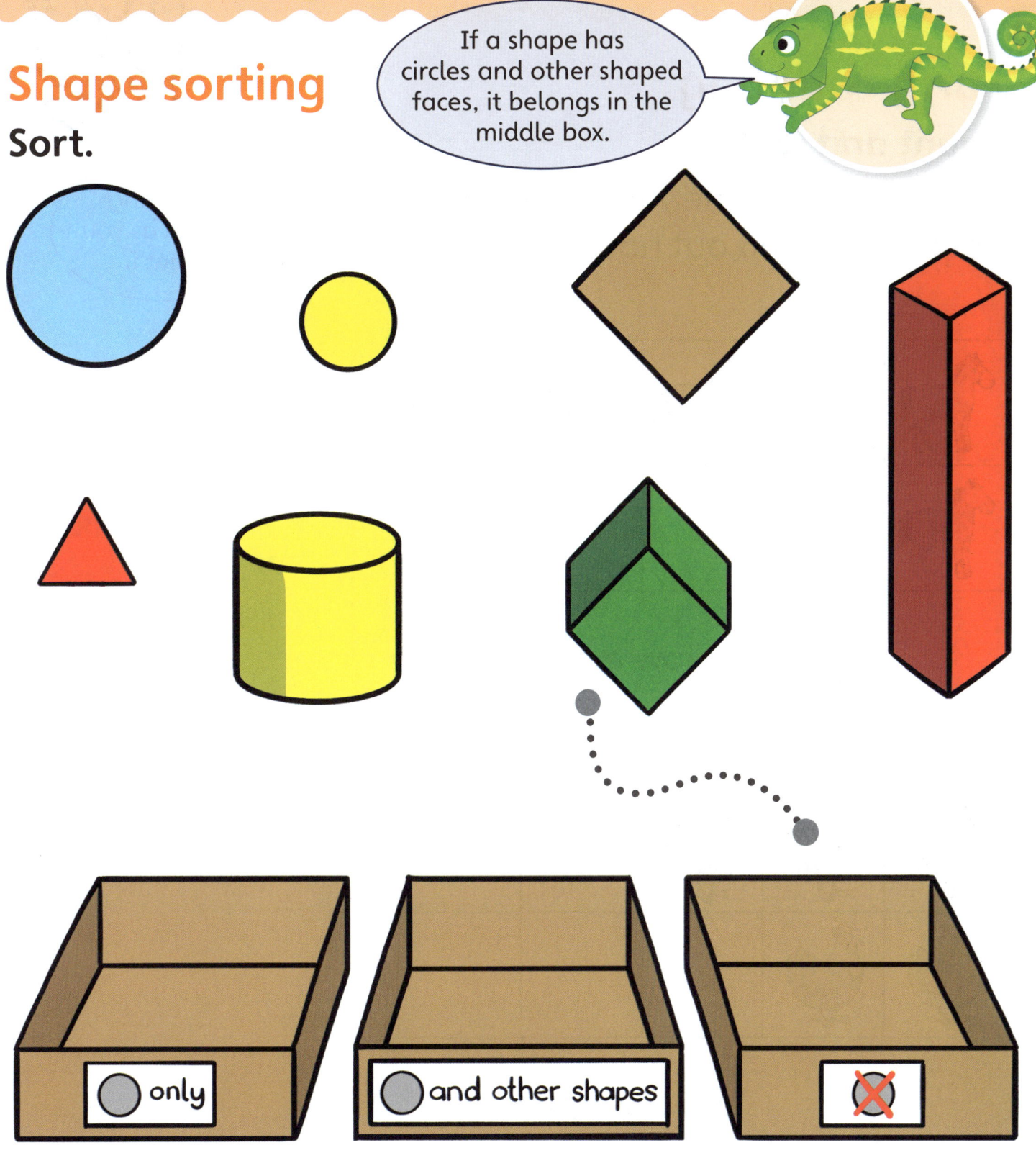

If a shape has circles and other shaped faces, it belongs in the middle box.

For practitioners
Encourage children to draw a line from each shape to the correct box. Some children will find it helpful to hold a circle and then look at each shape to see if it is a circle or has any circular faces. If children are unsure where a shape belongs, ask if it has any circular faces. If the answer is *no*, the shape belongs in the ❌ box. Challenge children to find an everyday object for each box.

Farm counting

Count and write.

Jamal is sorting the farm animal toys. Help him to find out how many there are.

Touch each animal as you count it.

How many horses?

How many chickens?

For practitioners

Invite children to count aloud as they touch count. Some children may recognise that a full row is 5, so there are 5 and 1 more horses: 6 horses. Challenge children to sort and say how many using some collections in the classroom. Give them some ten frames to check their counting.

Vehicle counting

Count and write.

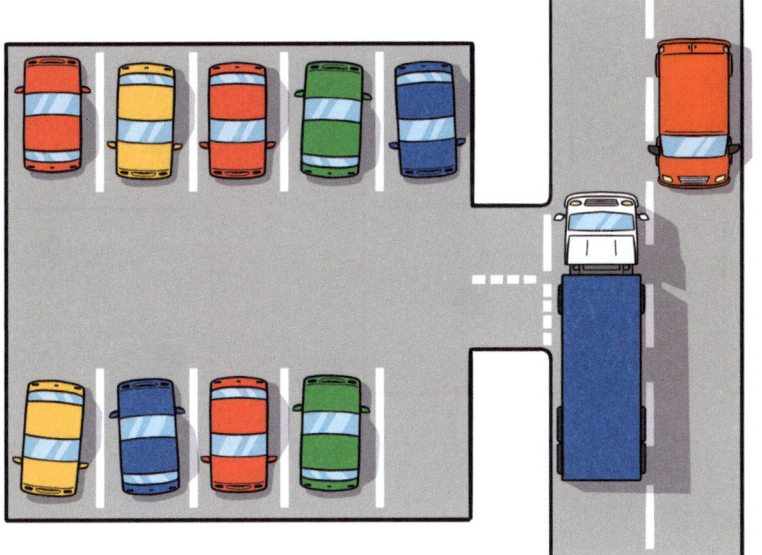

How many cars are in the car park?

How many motorbikes are in the car park?

For practitioners
Invite children to count aloud as they touch count. Some children may recognise that a full row is 5 and count on from there to find how many cars. Challenge children to count out a given number of cars, motorbikes, vans, fire engines or similar from the classroom vehicles. Give them some large ten frames to check their counting.

Domino numbers

Write.

How many spots are on each domino?

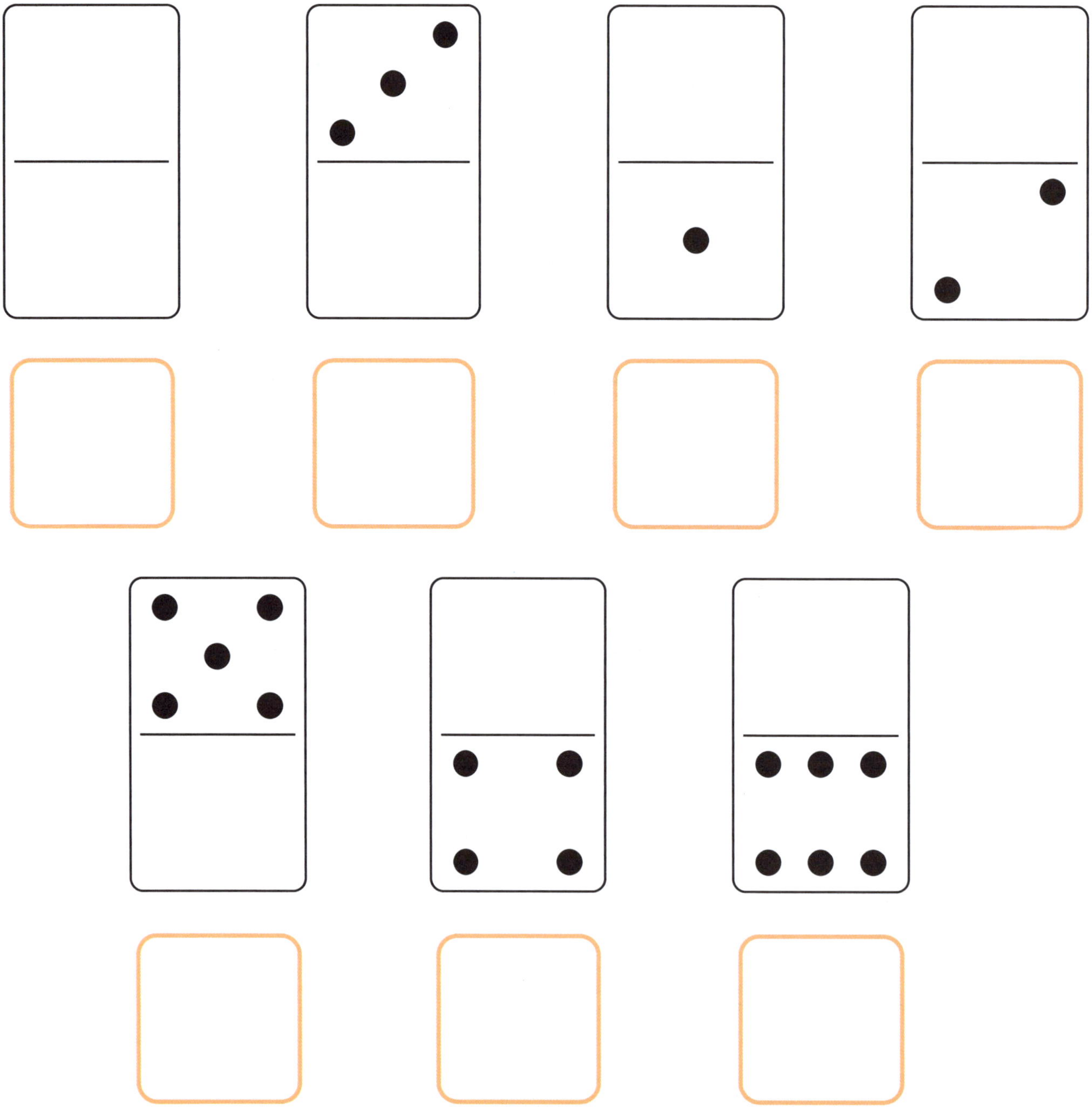

Can you say how many without counting?

For practitioners

Encourage children to write the number of spots, touching them if they cannot say how many without counting. Challenge children to find these dominoes from a set of dominoes.

Domino fours

Count and draw.

Each domino needs 4 spots altogether.
Make 3 different dominoes.

4   4   4

For practitioners
Give children 4 counters to arrange in different ways, for support. Dominoes could be 2–2, 1–3 or blank–4. Challenge children to find all the dominoes with a total of 6 spots from a set of dominoes.

Spot patterns

Count and colour.

Colour the matching number of spots on each Hungarian five frame.

You can choose any spots to colour. Count to check you have coloured the correct number of spots.

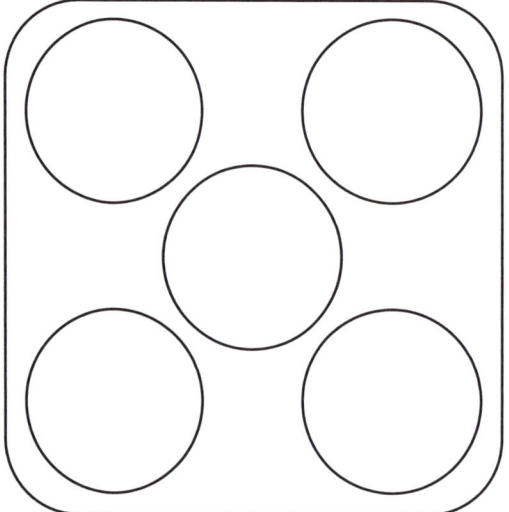

4

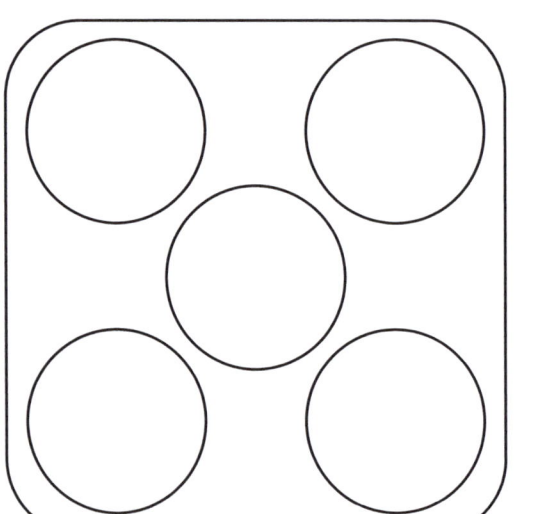

1

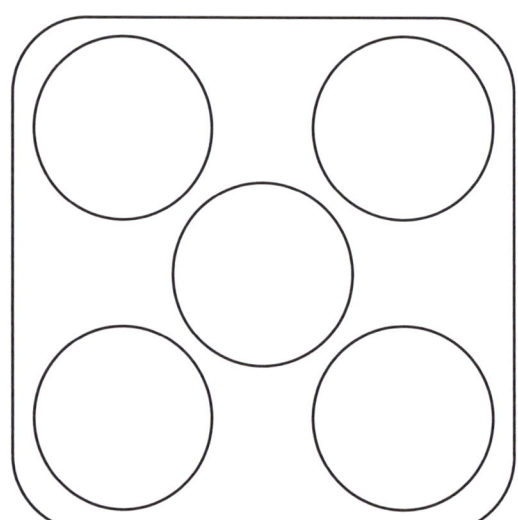

2

For practitioners

Encourage children to count the spots as they colour them. Any arrangement is correct if the indicated number of spots are coloured. Challenge children to say which numbers to 5 have not been represented (3 and 5) and to represent those numbers on 2 copies of the Hungarian five frame.

Make 6

Count and colour.

Show 6 in different ways.

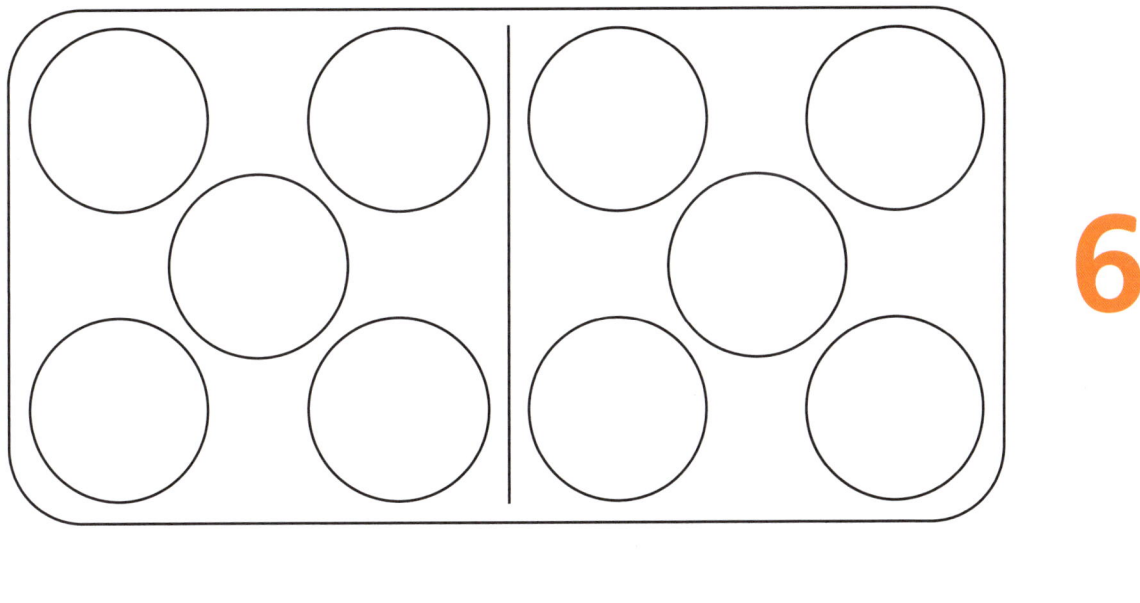

6

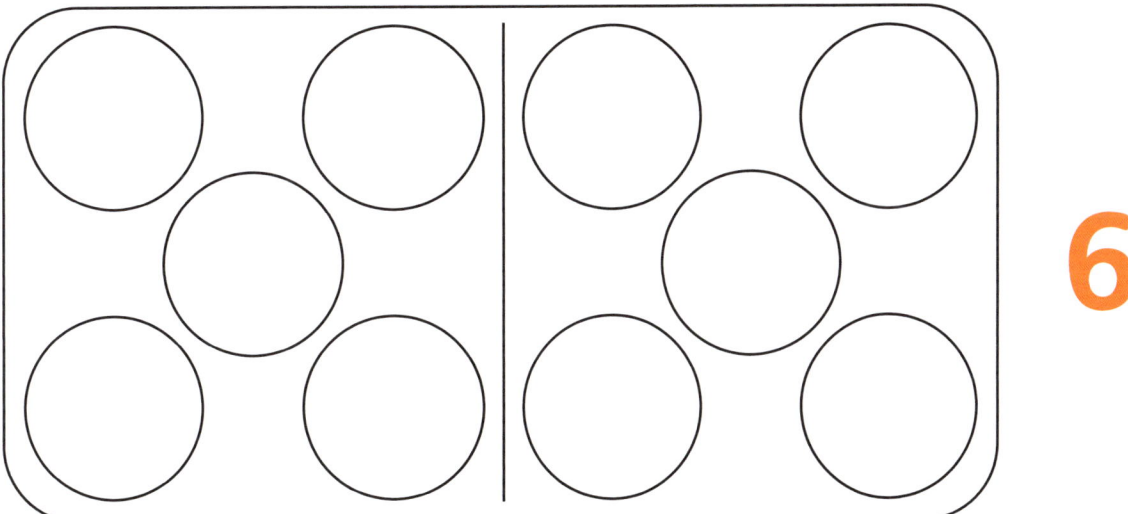

6

> **For practitioners**
> For support, children could count out 6 counters and place them on the Hungarian ten frame to help them choose which spots to colour. Challenge children to compare their 6s with a friend: How are they the same? How are they different?

Flower nines

Count and write.

Count and write the number in each vase.

_____ and _____ is equal to 9.

_____ and _____ is equal to 9.

_____ and _____ is equal to 9.

For practitioners

Encourage children to check that they have 9 flowers altogether.
Challenge children to draw 2 more pairs of vases to show more ways to equal 9 (9 and 0; 8 and 1).

Make 8

Draw and write.

Show 8 in different ways by drawing 2 different quantities on each ten frame.

_____ and _____ is equal to 8.

_____ and _____ is equal to 8.

_____ and _____ is equal to 8.

For practitioners
Give children some ideas of simple things to draw, for example, smiley faces, flowers, cookies, balls, butterflies, ice creams and so on. To make 2 quantities, children could draw 2 different things or the same thing in 2 different colours.

Block 4 — Wonderful water

Which has more?

Count, write and tick.

Which row in each box has more?

For practitioners

Encourage children to count and write the number of objects in each row. Some children may find it helpful to match each object with a counter to support their counting. Children compare the numbers in each pair of rows to find which row has more. They tick the row with more in each pair.

How many more?

Tick the frame that has more.

Count, write and tick.

Which ten frame in each box has more?

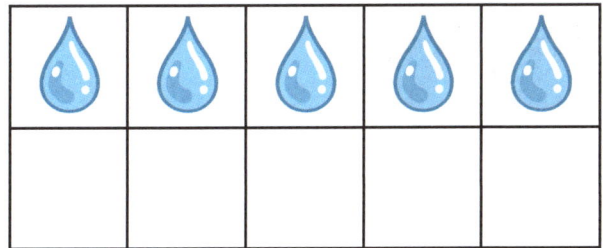
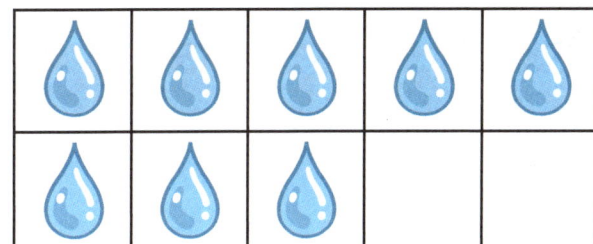

_____ _____

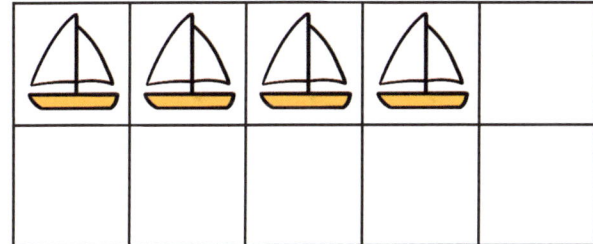

_____ _____

For practitioners

For each set, encourage children to count and write how many water drops or boats there are in each ten frame. Then ask *Which ten frame has more water drops (or boats)? How many more?* Some children may find it helpful to line up two sets of counters (or objects) to represent each group to work out how many more.

How many fewer?

Count, write and tick.

Which ten frame in each box has fewer?

Tick the frame that has fewer.

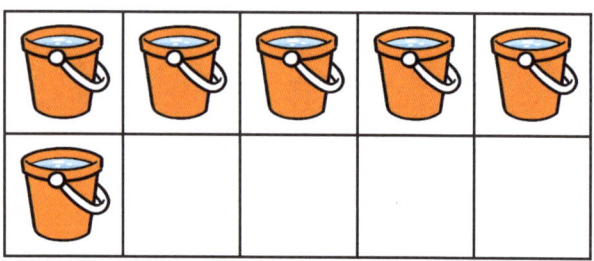 

For practitioners

For each set, encourage children to count and write how many buckets or umbrellas there are in each ten frame. Then ask *Which ten frame has fewer buckets (or umbrellas)? How many fewer?* Some children may find it helpful to line up two sets of counters (or objects) to represent each group to work out how many fewer.

How many ducks altogether?
Count and write.

Touch each duck as you count it.

2 ducks and 4 ducks equals _____ ducks.

For practitioners
Challenge children to make 2 groups using objects in the setting and count how many there are altogether.

How many flowers altogether?

Count, colour and write.

Touch each flower as you count it.

| 1 | 2 | 3 | 4 | 5 | 6 | 7 | 8 | 9 | 10 |

3 flowers and _____ flowers equals _____ flowers.

For practitioners
Encourage children to count the flowers then colour in the number on the track.
Challenge children to draw their own 2 groups of flowers and say how many flowers there are altogether.

Five frames

Draw.

Draw smiley faces ☺ on the five frames to show the totals.

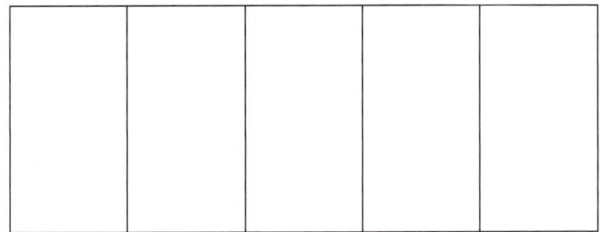 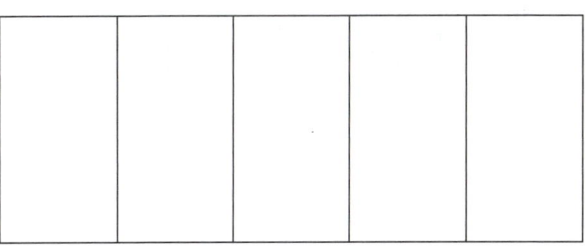 8

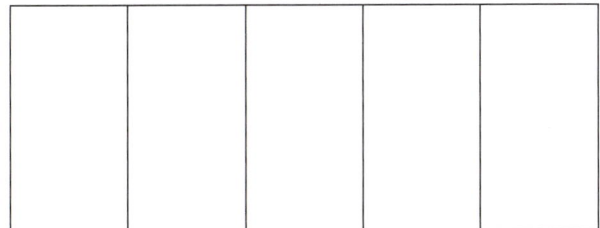 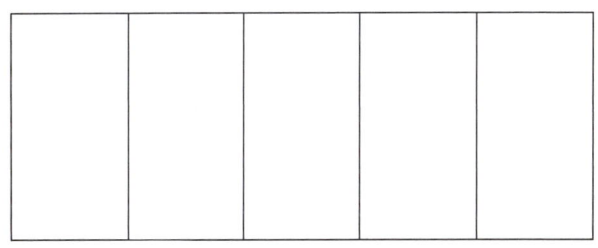 6

How many spaces are filled on each five frame?

For practitioners
Encourage children to complete one full five frame before moving onto the second one.

Fly away

Count and write.

Write the number of pelicans left in the pond when 3 pelicans fly away.

5 pelicans take away 3 pelicans is equal to _____ pelicans.

> **For practitioners**
> Encourage children to cross out 3 pelicans and count how many pelicans are left. Challenge children to make up their own pelican problems.

Cube sticks

Count and write.

How many cubes are left?

Cross out the cubes that are taken away, then count how many are left.

10 take away 4 is equal to _____.

10 take away 9 is equal to _____.

For practitioners

Encourage children to make the sticks with cubes if they find this difficult.
Challenge children to make their own stick of 10 cubes and explore taking away different quantities.

Taking away

Draw and write.

Draw a line across the strip to show 9 take away 4.

How many are left? _____

Draw a line across the strip to show 8 take away 6.

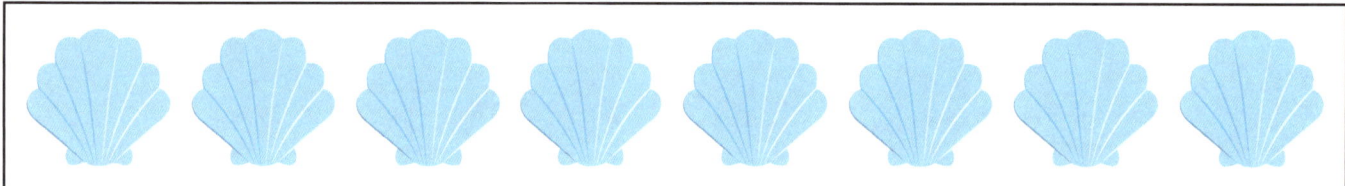

How many are left? _____

Draw a line across the strip to show 7 take away 2.

How many are left? _____

For practitioners
If children find this difficult, use sticks of cubes to match the strips.
Challenge children to make their own picture strips and explore taking away different quantities.

Patterns

Draw and say.

Continue the pattern in each row.

> Say the objects aloud so you can hear the pattern.

For practitioners

Challenge children to continue the pattern even further, either verbally or by drawing at least one more unit of repeat.

Flag patterns

Draw, colour and say.

Continue the pattern.

Say the colours aloud so you can hear the pattern.

For practitioners
Challenge children to continue the pattern, either verbally or by drawing and colouring in more shapes.

Spot the mistake
Circle and draw.

For practitioners
Encourage children to look at each pattern, spot the error and circle it. Challenge children to draw the correct pattern sequence underneath.

Complete the butterfly
Think and colour.

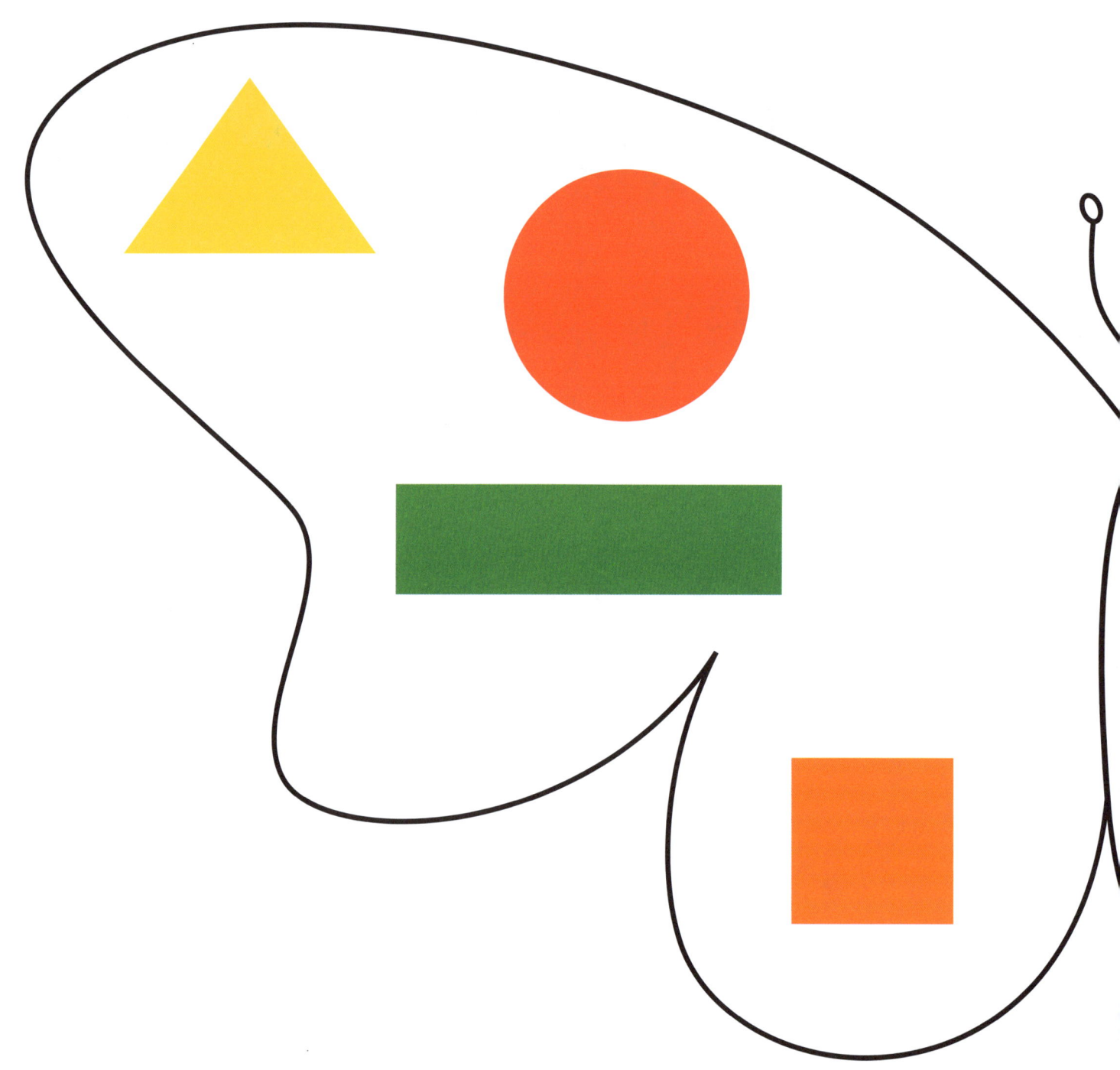

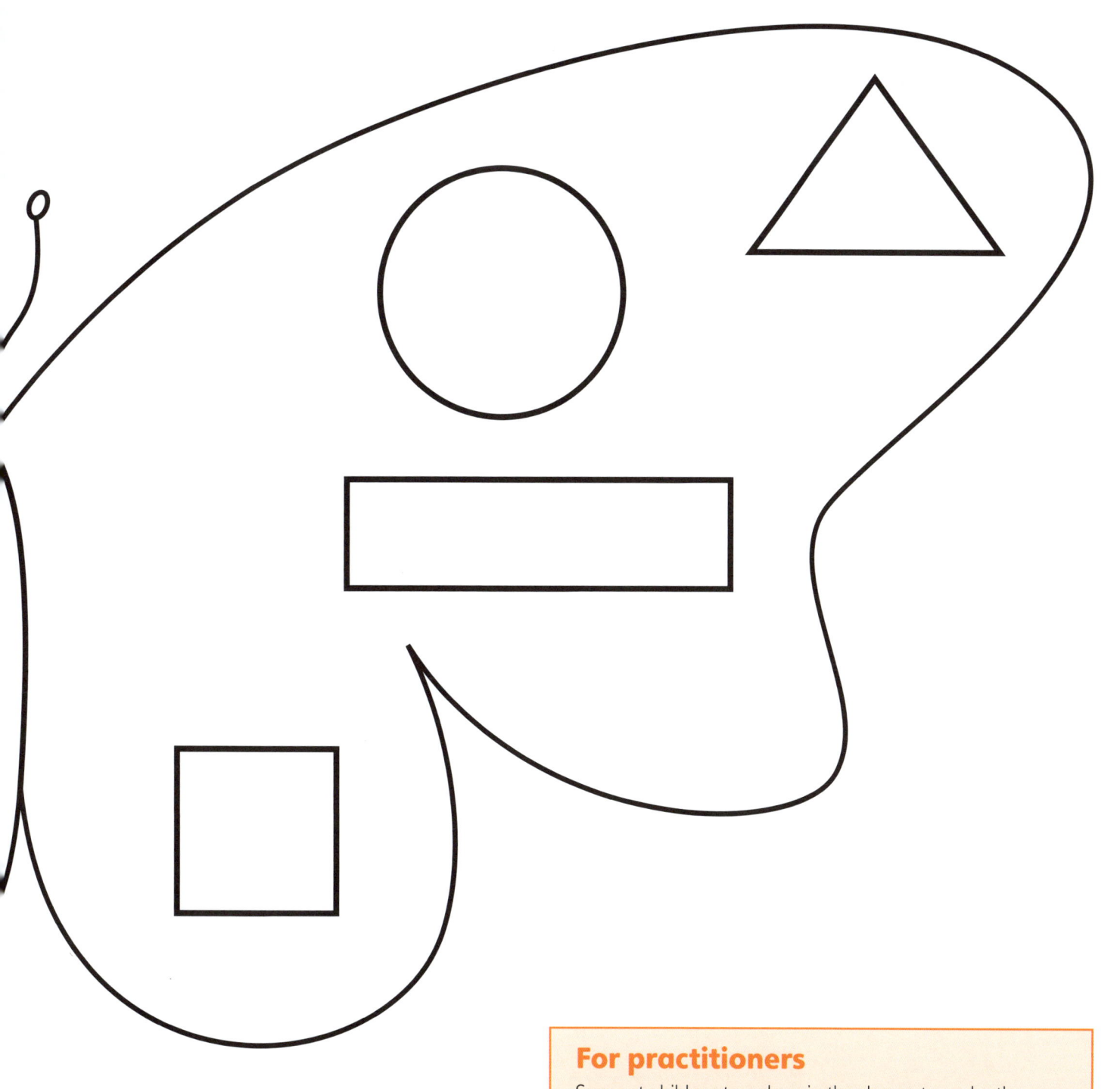

For practitioners
Support children to colour in the shapes to make the picture symmetrical. They could use a mirror to help them.

Acknowledgements

The authors and publishers acknowledge the following sources of copyright material and are grateful for the permissions granted.
While every effort has been made, it has not always been possible to identify the sources of all the material used, or to trace all copyright holders.
If any omissions are brought to our notice, we will be happy to include the appropriate acknowledgements on reprinting.

Thanks to the following artists at Beehive Illustration:

Laura Arias, Joe Wilkins.

Cover characters by Becky Davies (The Bright Agency)